Dear Parents:

Congratulations! Your child is taking the first steps on an exciting journey. The destination? Independent reading!

STEP INTO READING® will help your child get there. The program offers five steps to reading success. Each step includes fun stories and colorful art or photographs. In addition to original fiction and books with favorite characters, there are Step into Reading Non-Fiction Readers, Phonics Readers and Boxed Sets, Sticker Readers, and Comic Readers—a complete literacy program with something to interest every child.

Learning to Read, Step by Step!

Ready to Read   Preschool–Kindergarten
• big type and easy words • rhyme and rhythm • picture clues
For children who know the alphabet and are eager to begin reading.

Reading with Help   Preschool–Grade 1
• basic vocabulary • short sentences • simple stories
For children who recognize familiar words and sound out new words with help.

Reading on Your Own   Grades 1–3
• engaging characters • easy-to-follow plots • popular topics
For children who are ready to read on their own.

Reading Paragraphs   Grades 2–3
• challenging vocabulary • short paragraphs • exciting stories
For newly independent readers who read simple sentences with confidence.

Ready for Chapters   Grades 2–4
• chapters • longer paragraphs • full-color art
For children who want to take the plunge into chapter books but still like colorful pictures.

STEP INTO READING® is designed to give every child a successful reading experience. The grade levels are only guides; children will progress through the steps at their own speed, developing confidence in their reading.

Remember, a lifetime love of reading starts with a single step!

Step into Reading, Random House, and the Random House colophon are registered trademarks of Penguin Random House LLC.

Visit us on the Web!
StepIntoReading.com
randomhousekids.com

Educators and librarians, for a variety of teaching tools, visit us at RHTeachersLibrarians.com

ISBN 978-1-101-93855-3 (trade) — ISBN 978-1-101-93856-0 (lib. bdg.)

Printed in the United States of America   10 9 8 7 6 5 4 3 2 1

nickelodeon

TEENAGE MUTANT
NINJA TURTLES
OUT OF THE SHADOWS

SHELL
SHOCK

adapted by Geof Smith
illustrated by Paolo Villanelli

Based on the screenplay "Teenage Mutant Ninja Turtles: Out of the Shadows"
by Josh Appelbaum and André Nemec

Random House 🏠 New York

Four brothers protect
New York City.
They fight crime.

Their work is secret.
They hide
in the shadows.

They are
the Teenage Mutant
Ninja Turtles!

Their names are Leo,
Raph, Donnie, and Mikey.

Leo is the leader
of the Turtles.
He is the oldest brother.
Leo wants
to be a great ninja.

Watch out for Raph!
He is the biggest
and toughest Turtle.

He is very strong
and is not afraid
of a fight.

Donnie is the tallest.

He is very smart.

He makes all
the Turtles' gear.
He built their
awesome Turtle Van!

Mikey is always ready
to have fun.

He likes telling jokes
and eating pizza!

The wise rat Splinter
is the Turtles'
ninja master.

He teaches them
ninja moves.

Casey Jones helps
the Turtles fight crime.

He likes to stop
bad guys.
And he really likes
hockey!

Evil mutants threaten
New York City!
Bebop is
a giant warthog.

Rocksteady is
a powerful rhino.

The Turtles and Casey jump from the shadows!

They will stop
Bebop and Rocksteady!

Good guys rule!

It is pizza time!